Two Steps Forward

STUDY GUIDE

Sharon Garlough Brown

IVP Books

An imprint of InterVarsity Press
Downers Grove, Illinois

InterVarsity Press
P.O. Box 1400, Downers Grove, IL 60515-1426
ivpress.com
email@ivpress.com

InterVarsity Press® is the book-publishing division of InterVarsity Christian Fellowship/USA®, a movement of students and faculty active on campus at hundreds of universities, colleges, and schools of nursing in the United States of America, and a member movement of the International Fellowship of Evangelical Students. For information about local and regional activities, visit intervarsity.org.

Cover design: Cindy Kiple
Interior design: Daniel van Loon
Images: luggage: © monticelllo/iStockphoto
          four girls: © annie-claude/iStockphoto

ISBN 978-0-8308-4655-9 (print)
ISBN 978-0-8308-7033-2 (digital)

Printed in the United States of America ∞

InterVarsity Press is committed to ecological stewardship and to the conservation of natural resources in all our operations. This book was printed using sustainably sourced paper.

P	22	21	20	19	18	17	16	15	14	13	12	11	10	9	8	7	6	5	4
Y	38	37	36	35	34	33	32	31	30	29	28	27	26	25	24	23	22		

Contents

Introduction

The setting for *Two Steps Forward: A Story of Persevering in Hope* is the season of Advent, a season that invites us to keep watch and remain attentive to all the ways Christ comes into our world and our lives. Advent is a season of prayerful preparation, a season to practice hope—not the kind of hope that's synonymous with "wishing for" certain outcomes, but a hope firmly rooted in the person, work, and promises of God in Jesus Christ.

Sybil MacBeth, author of *The Season of the Nativity: Confessions and Practices of an Advent, Christmas, and Epiphany Extremist*, writes,

> During Advent we are reminded of the paradoxes and incongruities of life: light and darkness; faith and fear; joy and sorrow; vulnerability and power; weakness and strength; done, but not complete; already and not yet. These pairs of contrasting ideas are not just for Advent. They are the daily themes and dilemmas of ordinary, everyday Christians—the people who believe that an embodied, flesh-and-blood Messiah has already come, but that the transformation of the world is not yet complete.

We are called to be Advent people, to live in a posture of readiness and expectation, every day of the year.

This study guide is not an "Advent guide" (though it could be adapted for use during Advent), but rather an eight-week journey in spiritual formation, using the book's characters as windows and mirrors for better understanding our own life with God, our receptivity and resistance, our longings and fears, and our two steps forward and frequent steps back. Each week you'll find daily Scripture readings and reflection questions as well as a spiritual practice to integrate into your rhythm of life. This guide also includes group discussion questions and exercises to explore and practice in community. (Please note, if you are using the guide with a group, week seven is an invitation to serve together, which may require advance planning.)

You can decide whether to read *Two Steps Forward* first in its entirety and then return to do a slow study with the guide, or to read it a section at a time, matching your pace to the daily questions. I recommend keeping a travelogue of your journey. Even if you aren't in the habit of using a journal, you'll benefit from having a record of what you're noticing as you move forward.

Not every question will resonate with you. That's okay. You don't need to answer every question every day. But do watch for any impulse to avoid a question because it agitates you or makes you feel uncomfortable. That's probably the very question you need to spend time pondering! If you don't have time to answer the questions you want to reflect on, simply mark them and return on the review days. If something in the chapter speaks to you and isn't addressed in a question, spend time journaling and praying about it.

Christ has come. Christ still comes to us. Christ will come again. May the Spirit prepare and enable you to receive Christ daily, in the midst of the challenges and the joys, with wonder and gratitude and hope.

Sharon Garlough Brown

*Now to him who is able to do immeasurably more than
all we ask or imagine, according to his power that is at work within us,
to him be glory in the church and in Christ Jesus throughout
all generations, for ever and ever! Amen.*

(EPHESIANS 3:20-21)

Reading for Week One:
Prologue and Chapters One and Two

Meg practices breath prayer as a way to center herself in God's presence and to be continually reminded that God is with her. This week practice matching a short prayer to your rhythm of breathing. You might choose a verse and divide it into an inhale-exhale pattern. For example: "Be still [inhale], and know that I am God [exhale]" (Psalm 46:10). Or choose a name for God from Scripture and then express a brief declaration of faith, petition, or desire. Examples: "Emmanuel [inhale], you are with me [exhale]." "Author of life [inhale], renew me in your love [exhale]."

Spend time listening for a prayer. How is God inviting you to name him? What does God invite you to declare about who he is or what you need? As you breathe, receive the very breath of God enlivening you. Practice being attentive to your breathing throughout the day so that prayer becomes habitual.

. . . .

Week One: Day One

∞

PROLOGUE (P. 9)

Scripture Meditation: Hebrews 10:24-25
Slowly read the text out loud a few times, listening for a word or phrase that catches your attention and invites you to linger with it in prayer (lectio divina). How does this particular word or phrase connect with your life? How does it comfort or confront you? Talk with God about your response to this word, your thoughts and feelings that arise. Then listen for God's invitations to you. Finish with a time of silence, resting in God's presence.

For Reflection and Journaling

1. Who are your trustworthy companions on the spiritual journey? Give God thanks for the gift of community and for the ways you have been shaped, encouraged, and challenged (even provoked) by others.

2. How is God inviting you to pray for your fellow travelers? Who do you need to release to God's care today?

3. If you have struggled to find or connect in community, offer your longings, fears, or hurts to God in prayer. Ask God to guide you toward someone who can walk with you.

Week One: Day Two

CHAPTER ONE: *MEG AND CHARISSA* (PP. 13-25)

Scripture Meditation: 1 Peter 5:7
Read the verse aloud a few times. Then match it with the palms down/palms up prayer (described in *Sensible Shoes*). With your palms down, release your cares and concerns to God. With your palms up, receive God's care and concern for you.

For Reflection and Journaling

1. What comes to mind when you think about the word *hope*? What helps you persevere in hope? As you move forward with this study, light a hope candle when you pray as a declaration of God's presence with you.

2. How do you feel about detours and surprises? Recall a significant detour in your own life. How did you navigate it? How did God reveal himself in the midst of it (or afterward)?

3. In what ways do you struggle to let go of control and trust God? What helps you practice this?

. . . .

Week One: Day Three

∞

CHAPTER ONE: *HANNAH AND MARA* (PP. 26-39)

Scripture Meditation: Romans 15:13
Read the verse slowly and prayerfully several times. Which word or phrase catches your attention and invites your pondering and response to God?

For Reflection and Journaling

1. Hannah has spent years being overly responsible, hiding behind her busyness, thriving on being needed, and finding her security and

significance in her work. Do you share anything in common with her? Speak to God about what you notice.

2. Do you regularly practice rest and play? If not, spend time identifying both the external and internal obstacles to practicing it. How might you incorporate celebration and rest into your rhythm of life?

3. Mara looks at the landscape of her life and wonders, "What can be born in a place like this?" Spend time considering the landscape of your own life. How are you welcoming Christ's presence into chaos, trials, or mess?

Week One: Day Four

CHAPTER TWO: MEG (PP. 40-47 AND 53-60)

Scripture Meditation: Matthew 1:21-23
Read the verses aloud several times. What does it mean for you to call Jesus "Immanuel"? Spend time quietly receiving him as "God with us." What is your prayer?

For Reflection and Journaling
1. Meg contemplates the ways God provides for her through the kindness of strangers—even a stranger she was ready to dismiss as strange. Bring to mind some situations in which God has demonstrated his care and provision for you (perhaps in unexpected ways). How has God shown that

he is "God with you"? How might remembering this affect the ways you trust that God is with you now?

2. Recall a time when you experienced profound disappointment. What were the circumstances? Are you able to see any ways God met you in the midst of them, demonstrating he was "God with you"?

3. Meg prays, "O come, O come, Emmanuel, and ransom me from my captivity." In what ways are you captive? In what ways are you longing for freedom? Offer Emmanuel what you notice, and ask for his rescue.

....

Week One: Day Five

CHAPTER TWO: *HANNAH* (PP. 48-52)

Scripture Meditation: Isaiah 9:2-4
Read the verses slowly several times. Which word or phrase catches your attention and evokes your prayerful response?

For Reflection and Journaling
Use Hannah's journal questions as your own today.

1. In what ways is the light coming and shining into places where you have dwelt in darkness? How do you respond to the light and what it reveals?

2. What are the yokes that God is longing to break in your life? What burdens do you carry on your shoulders that God is trying to remove and carry for you?

3. How will you practice releasing these burdens and receiving God?

. . . .

Week One: Day Six

REVIEW

1. In the opening chapters of *Two Steps Forward*, we catch a glimpse of some of the ongoing battles for the characters: fear, grief, envy, self-centeredness, anxiety, discouragement, holding on to control, lacking trust in God, and struggling to rest. In what specific ways do you identify with the women? Offer what you notice to God in prayer.

2. Prayerfully review your notes from this week. Do you glimpse any emerging patterns of receptivity or resistance? Speak with God about what you notice.

3. How has the practice of breath prayer impacted, challenged, or blessed you this week?

Week One Group Discussion

If the group is new, discuss boundaries and expectations. Commit to giving one another the gift of confidentiality. Offer compassionate, attentive listening. Group leaders should determine time parameters each week for discussion questions. If possible, light a candle to remind yourselves that you're in the presence of God together.

Optional icebreaker: Who is your favorite character? Least favorite? Why?

1. Discuss some of the struggles that are evident in the lives of the characters. In what specific ways do you identify with them?

2. Read Isaiah 9:2-4. Then discuss some of your insights from journaling about light, yokes, and burdens (day five) this week.

3. Share your breath prayer with the group. What fruit do you notice from practicing it this week?

4. How can the group pray for you as you move forward in hope?

Reading for Week Two:
Chapters Three and Four

SPIRITUAL PRACTICE: EXAMEN

Meg practices prayerfully reviewing her day with God, noticing and naming the moments when she was aware of the presence of God and the moments when God seemed hidden, moments when she responded with faith and moments when she was overcome by fear.

This week try giving ten to twenty minutes each day for prayerfully reviewing the past twenty-four hours. The prayer of examen is typically practiced at the end of the day, but choose a time that best suits your rhythm and schedule.

Begin the prayer by quieting yourself in the presence of God, giving God thanks for some of the gifts of the day. Then ask the Holy Spirit to help you notice and name how God has been with you and how you have been with God. In what ways have you recognized God's presence today? In what ways has God seemed hidden? How have you moved toward God or away from God today? In what ways have you been brought to life or depleted?

Having pondered these things, spend time responding to what you've seen. Celebrate God's goodness to you. Confess what needs to be confessed and receive God's grace and forgiveness. Grieve what needs to be grieved and receive God's comfort. In light of what you've noticed in your prayerful review of the day, how might you live tomorrow differently? What will help you be more attentive and responsive to the Spirit of God? (For a more detailed teaching on the prayer of examen, see *Sensible Shoes*.)

Week Two: Day One

Chapter Three: *Charissa* (pp. 61-69)

Scripture Meditation: Luke 1:26-38
Read the passage aloud. What thoughts and emotions are stirred in you as you ponder Mary's response? Offer what you notice to God in prayer.

For Reflection and Journaling

1. Dr. Allen encourages his students to offer what's true, not what's impressive. How honest are you with yourself, God, and others about your sin, struggles, and weaknesses? Why?

2. Charissa contemplates the contrast between Mary's obedient surrender to the formation of the Son of God within her and her own resistance to the formation of life within her (both physically and spiritually). Use Charissa's questions for your own reflection: Are you ready to say a fully surrendered *yes* to the kind of Life that changes everything? Or do you prefer a less intimate, less intrusive Presence you can follow from a comfortable distance? Speak honestly to God about your resistance and receptivity.

3. Dr. Allen encourages Charissa to name the things that have died: her plans, ambitions, and vision of life. "These spiritual and emotional deaths are no less significant than the physical ones, but they can be harder to name" (p. 65). Are there any deaths for you to name and grieve right now? Offer to God the truth about what you see.

4. What helps you create sacred space where the life of Christ can flourish and grow?

....

Week Two: Day Two

CHAPTER THREE: *MEG* (PP. 70-73)

Scripture Meditation: Isaiah 43:1
Read the verse slowly and prayerfully. Imagine God calling you by name and speaking the words to you. What is your response?

For Reflection and Journaling

1. Which are you quicker to notice and name: gifts or challenges? Why? How does the examen help you see God in the midst of both?

2. Do you typically stuff, deny, and fight your fears or offer them to God? Spend time offering fears and worries to him. (Use the palms down/palms up prayer if helpful.)

3. What helps you focus on the love and presence of God when you feel afraid, overwhelmed, or disappointed?

....

Week Two: Day Three

CHAPTER THREE: MARA (PP. 74-88)

Scripture Meditation: Luke 1:26-38
Read the passage aloud slowly, imagining yourself as Mary. What do you see? Hear? Feel? Think? How would you respond to the angel's message? Speak with God about what you notice.

For Reflection and Journaling

1. Katherine invites Mara to name what is true, even when the honesty "sounds ugly." How honest and unedited are you in your prayers? If you were convinced God would not punish you for being candid about your thoughts and feelings, what would you pray? Spend time writing the words, speaking the words, and asking for the courage to pray the words. Take the exercise one step further by identifying a trusted companion and confessing your honest thoughts, feelings, fears, struggles, or sin aloud.

2. Mara struggles to believe she is chosen, loved, and favored. So Katherine points out that the Greek word for "favored" in Luke 1:28 means "graced." In fact, the apostle Paul uses the same word in Ephesians 1:6 to describe God pouring out his grace on us: "to the praise of his glorious grace that he *freely bestowed* on us in the Beloved" (NRSV; emphasis mine). Journal about your own response to the word "favored." What helps you receive the good news of God's grace? What makes it hard to believe? Practice standing in front of a mirror and saying these words: "Greetings, favored one! The Lord is with you!" Note your receptivity or resistance to the exercise.

3. Identify some of your own "how can it be" questions. "How can it be since I'm [fill in the blank with whatever you think is going to make it impossible for God to do what he says he's going to do in you, for you, and through you]?" Offer your wonder, perplexity, and fears to God in prayer.

···

Week Two: Day Four

CHAPTER FOUR: CHARISSA, MEG, AND HANNAH (PP. 89-97)

Scripture Meditation: Luke 1:26-38
Read the text aloud, listening for a word or phrase that catches your attention and calls for your prayerful response. Speak to God about what you notice.

For Reflection and Journaling

1. How do you navigate disappointment? What are God's invitations to you in the midst of disappointments?

2. Ponder what it means to be "pregnant with the Son of God," to be chosen, graced, and favored to bear Christ like Mary. Find a way to celebrate the Spirit's work in making you a dwelling place for the Most High God, "like a womb where Jesus is being formed. . . . Not just a place where Jesus has to be born because there's no room somewhere else. But a place God chooses" (p. 97). What helps you receive and believe that good news?

3. Hannah realizes she has some grieving to do. She recognizes that the Holy Spirit is trying to catch her attention by pressing on wounded places, so she names her sorrow in prayer. In what ways are you being invited to "linger with what provokes you"? Is there any grief to be named to God in prayer? Any wound of sorrow that has become infected with self-pity, bitterness, or resentment? Write a prayer of lament, offering God your honest thoughts, feelings, pain, or disappointment.

....

Week Two: Day Five

CHAPTER FOUR: *MARA AND CHARISSA* (PP. 98-103)

Scripture Meditation: Romans 8:1-4
Read the passage in several different translations. Are there any declarations that are difficult for you to believe? Why? Offer your response to God in prayer.

For Reflection and Journaling

1. Mara is beginning to see that her awareness of temptation and wrestling is part of her progress forward. In what ways are you becoming quicker to recognize gravitational pulls toward sin, shame, or condemnation? How might this awareness encourage you?

2. What would it mean for you to use the thorn of the accuser's voice as a reminder to turn to Jesus for help and grace? How can you practice this even now?

3. Charissa wonders if the possibility of miscarriage is her fault. Have you ever had similar questions about a circumstance in your life? What conclusions did you draw in the end? Have a conversation with God about this.

Week Two: Day Six

REVIEW

1. Prayerfully review your notes from this week. Do you glimpse any emerging patterns of receptivity or resistance? Speak with God about what you notice.

2. How has the practice of the examen impacted, challenged, or blessed you this week?

Week Two Group Discussion

If possible, light a candle to remind yourselves that you are in the presence of God together. Open with a few minutes for silent breath prayer. Then speak Katherine's prayer together: "Lord, you have made your home in us; may we make ourselves at home in you" (p. 77).

1. Many of your reflection questions this week focused on Luke 1:26-38. Read this passage aloud, then discuss your experiences of praying with the text this week. Or practice lectio divina or praying with imagination together.

2. Share one insight from praying the examen this week. How are you being shaped or challenged by the practice?

3. Which parts of the characters' journeys this week resonated with you or challenged you? Why?

4. As a way of offering God's blessing to one another, take turns speaking these words to the person on your left: "Do not be afraid, [name], for you have found favor with God." Be sure to take time to listen to and savor the blessing when it is spoken to you.

Reading for Week Three:
Chapters Five and Six

SPIRITUAL PRACTICE: WAITING

One of the common ways God forms us is through our waiting. If you find it difficult to wait—if, like Nathan, you find yourself battling impatience while waiting—look for opportunities this week to practice waiting well. If you choose to wait in the longest line at the grocery store, don't distract yourself with a phone or magazine while you wait. Use the time to be attentive to the presence of God. What would God have you notice about the people around you? How might you pray for them? Offer a word of kindness? Provide a simple act of service? Practice prayerfulness in the waiting times. Keep a record of what you notice about your waiting.

Reflect, too, on seasons of waiting in your life. How did God meet you, shape you, or stretch you while you waited? How might these recollections affect the way you wait now or in the future?

Finally, consider others who are in a season of waiting right now. How might you encourage, support, or pray for them while they wait?

....

Week Three: Day One

∞

CHAPTER FIVE: *MARA* (PP. 107-113)

Scripture Meditation: Ephesians 4:25
Read the verse slowly and prayerfully. In what ways are you challenged by it? Encouraged by it? How is God calling you to live it?

For Reflection and Journaling

1. Hannah remembers wounding Mara by manipulating her into self-disclosure and asks for her forgiveness. Ask God to bring to mind anyone you have wounded by your sin. Do you have the opportunity to ask for forgiveness? If so, what keeps you from seeking it? Speak to God about what you notice and pray for courage and wisdom as you move forward.

2. What circumstances or people has God used in your life to bring to the surface unresolved pain? Who has helped (or is helping) you process this? Who loves you enough to ask important (and sometimes difficult) questions? Speak to God about what you notice.

3. Hannah names her tendency to compare and measure her own suffering against what others endure, telling herself she "shouldn't feel bad because so-and-so has it so much worse" (p. 112). Have you ever been tempted to deny or minimize your own pain? Why? What was the result? Make an offering of any buried, potentially toxic pain to God in prayer.

. . . .

Week Three: Day Two

CHAPTER FIVE: HANNAH (PP. 114-121)

Scripture Meditation: Romans 5:1-5
Read the text aloud a few times, listening for a word or phrase that catches your attention and opens you to prayer. Speak with God about what you notice. Listen for his response.

For Reflection and Journaling

1. How did you enjoy playing as a child? If nothing specific comes to mind, imagine a time of play that would bring you joy. How could you pursue this, in solitude or in community?

2. When Hannah tells Nathan she intends to practice fasting from something that gives her joy, he challenges her. For Hannah, feasting is more difficult than fasting, and Nathan believes she will derive greater spiritual benefit from practicing celebration than practicing self-denial. What about you? Are you more practiced with feasting or fasting? What might God be calling you to practice right now? What do you hope the fruit will be?

3. What has suffering produced in you? Do any of Hannah's reflections on Romans 5:1-5 (pp. 120-121) resonate with you? In what ways?

4. What are you waiting for today? What is your prayer while you wait?

....

Week Three: Day Three

∞

CHAPTER FIVE: *MEG* (PP. 122-130)

Scripture Meditation: Daniel 2:20-22
Read the text slowly a couple of times. Which particular declarations about God speak to you right now? Why? What is your prayer?

For Reflection and Journaling

1. What do you notice about Meg's interactions with Becca in London? In what ways is she stuck in old patterns? Trying to move forward? Do any of her struggles resonate with you? Why or why not?

2. What helps you discern whether your motives are self-centered or rooted in love? How have regrets or fears affected the quality of your relationships with those close to you? Offer your response to God.

3. How is God revealing deep and hidden things to you right now? How do you feel about what you see? Speak honestly to God about this.

....

Week Three: Day Four

CHAPTER SIX: *CHARISSA, MEG, AND MARA* (PP. 131-148)

Scripture Meditation: Romans 12:15
Read the verse aloud several times. Which is easier for you: rejoicing with those who rejoice or weeping with those who weep? Why? What is your prayer?

For Reflection and Journaling

1. Some of the characters are experiencing significant stress and conflict in relationships. Are there any relationships in your life that need particular attention and prayer right now? What active steps toward reconciliation are possible or necessary?

2. Is there anyone alongside you to offer support and encouragement in the midst of heartache or stress? What truth are you being invited to speak— to God, others, or yourself?

3. What kinds of trials typically cause you to second-guess your decisions or doubt God's love and favor? Speak with God about what you notice.

....

Week Three: Day Five

⌒

CHAPTER SIX: HANNAH (PP. 149-154)

Scripture Meditation: John 1:1-9

Read John 1:1-9 slowly and prayerfully several times out loud. Which word or phrase captures your attention and invites you to ponder it? How does this word or phrase connect with your life? What feelings or thoughts arise concerning this word? Offer your response to God in prayer; listen for God's invitation and response to you. Finish with a time of silence, resting in the presence of God.

For Reflection and Journaling

1. Who is God calling you to walk alongside during a difficult season? How will you pray, listen, keep watch, and trust God's coming in the midst of the mess? How is this posture different from trying to fix, rescue, or give advice?

2. Nathan speaks to Hannah about the ways he "lost [his] soul trying to be everything for everyone else while neglecting [his] own life with God" (p. 151). Do you share anything in common with him? If so, what?

3. Read John 1:20. Think about any ways in which you have tried to be the Messiah, the rescuer. What is at the root of the impulse to intervene and try to manage God's world for him? Write a resignation letter to God. If you're comfortable, read your resignation letter aloud to your group or a trusted friend.

Week Three: Day Six

REVIEW

1. Prayerfully review your notes from this week. Do you glimpse any emerging patterns or themes? Speak with God about what you notice.

2. How has the practice of waiting impacted, challenged, or shaped you this week? In what ways were you enabled to wait well? In what ways did you grow impatient with waiting? What is your prayer?

Week Three Group Discussion

If possible, light a candle to remind yourselves that you are in the presence of God together. This week, begin with a word of grace and blessing. Gather in a circle and take turns speaking these words to the person on your right: "Do not be afraid, [name], for you have found favor with God." Be sure to take time to listen to and savor the blessing when it is spoken to you.

1. Share one thing you noticed about waiting this week. How can you wait together in hope?

2. Practice group lectio divina. Choose four different readers and read John 1:1-9, with a few minutes of silence between each reading. Which word or phrase captures your attention as you listen? In silence, spend time journaling your prayerful responses to God's Word.

Group leaders: offer approximately twenty minutes, allowing members enough time to quietly reflect on the Scripture text. When people have finished journaling, ask, "What came to life for you as you prayed with the Word?" Make sure each group member has the opportunity to share, if desired.

3. Read aloud your resignation letters, if you're comfortable sharing. After each group member reads, pause and offer silent prayer, asking God to receive the releasing of control.

4. In closing prayer, let each person offer a one-sentence declaration of longing or need to God. Pause in silence after each declaration is offered, asking God to draw near and reveal his presence.

Reading for Week Four: Chapters Seven and Eight

SPIRITUAL PRACTICE: GUIDANCE

God promises to supply wisdom when we lack it (James 1:5), to counsel us with his eye on us (Psalm 32:8), to direct our paths (Proverbs 3:5-6), and to speak with a Shepherd's voice (John 10:27). This week spend time considering how you receive guidance from God. What is the role of community in the process? Which Scripture texts are significant to you as you think about being guided by God?

If you are currently seeking guidance, think about a past experience of seeking God for direction. How did God reveal his way to you? Does your current experience share anything in common with your past experience? Watch for recurring themes or patterns in the ways God has guided you. Journal your insights.

....

Week Four: Day One

CHAPTER SEVEN: *MEG* (PP. 155-164)

Scripture Meditation: Psalm 25:4-10
Read the passage aloud a few times. In what ways does this ancient prayer echo your own needs and longings? Speak it to God as a prayer for yourself and others.

For Reflection and Journaling

1. Name some of the fresh grief and disappointments for Meg. Do any of her heartaches resonate with you? Why or why not?

2. What does love look like when you don't condone or approve of someone's choices? How have you faced this challenge in your own life?

3. Meg writes, "I don't know what to do, Lord. And I don't know how I'm going to hear Your voice when the voices inside my head are so noisy" (p. 164). Have you ever experienced similar frustration and confusion? How did Emmanuel meet you? What is your prayer now?

. . . .

Week Four: Day Two

CHAPTER SEVEN: *MARA AND HANNAH* (PP. 165-172)

Scripture Meditation: Matthew 10:16
Read the verse aloud a few times, listening for a word or phrase that catches your attention and calls for your response. How is the Spirit stirring you with Jesus' words?

For Reflection and Journaling

1. Life continues to unravel for Mara. Do you find yourself hoping for a particular outcome in her situation at home? If so, what do your longings for her reveal about your longings for yourself or for those you love who are in the midst of trials? Offer your observations to God in prayer.

2. If you were alongside Mara as a friend, what concerns would you have? What would you say? What would you not say? How would you pray?

3. For the first time in her life, Mara is experiencing the gift of community, a reminder that God is with her in the midst of the mess. Bring to mind a time of suffering in your own life. What role did community play throughout the trial, either in sharing your burden or compounding your pain? Offer what you notice to God.

. . . .

Week Four: Day Three

CHAPTER EIGHT: *CHARISSA* (PP. 173-181 AND 187-188)

Scripture Meditation: Hebrews 12:11-13
Read the verses slowly, listening for a word or phrase that catches your attention and invites you to linger. What is your prayer?

For Reflection and Journaling

1. Have you ever experienced the sort of shame and humiliation Charissa feels after missing her presentation? If so, what were the circumstances? How did you view the situation then? What about now? Speak with God about what you notice.

2. John tries to talk to Charissa about her reaction. If you were alongside her, what would you say to her? How might she respond? Why?

3. What does Charissa conclude about how Christ is being formed in her? Do you share anything in common with her? If so, in what ways? Offer your honest response to God.

Week Four: Day Four

CHAPTER EIGHT: *MARA* (PP. 182-184)

Scripture Meditation: John 10:10-11
Read the verses slowly and prayerfully. Where have you seen evidence of the thief's work? What about the work of the Good Shepherd? What is your prayer?

For Reflection and Journaling

1. How would you describe Mara's state of mind and heart after she receives the legal paperwork? What do you see that concerns you? Encourages you? Why?

2. Think back to a decision you regret. What motivated you at the time? What fruit resulted from the decision? What would you change now if you could? Speak with God about what you see.

3. How would you define an "empty life"? What makes for a full life? Be honest in your definitions. Then offer your longings to God in prayer.

....

Week Four: Day Five

∞

CHAPTER EIGHT: HANNAH (PP. 185-186)

Scripture Meditation: 1 Corinthians 16:13-14
Read the verses aloud, listening for a word or phrase that stirs your thoughts or emotions. What is your prayer?

For Reflection and Journaling

1. Nate defines discernment as taking the next faithful step, guided by love. How would you define *discernment*?

2. Hannah identifies a difference between putting confidence in her ability to hear God and putting confidence in God's ability to speak in a way she can understand. Does this feel like a paradigm shift for you? If so, spend some time processing it. What difference would such a posture shift make for you?

3. Identify times in your life when you were driven by fear, guilt, or duty. What was the result? Identify times in your life when you were guided by love. What was the fruit? What is love calling you to do right now?

Week Four: Day Six

REVIEW

1. Prayerfully review your notes from this week. In what ways were you challenged? Comforted? Frustrated? Inspired? How have you seen Emmanuel revealed this week? Speak with God about what you notice.

2. What have you noticed about the ways God has guided you in the past? How has God demonstrated his presence with you? How does this encourage you as you move forward?

Week Four Group Discussion

If possible, light a candle to remind yourselves that you are in the presence of God together. Invite a few readers to take turns reading Psalm 23 as you begin. Then give space for silent pondering and prayer.

1. Discuss any points of resonance with the characters' unfolding journeys. Who are you sympathetic or frustrated with? Why? In what ways are the characters providing windows to glimpse God and others more clearly, or mirrors to see yourself?

2. What comes to mind when you think about the "ministry of presence"? In what ways is your group practicing this? How can you be more intentional about authentic, compassionate community?

3. What did you notice as you explored the practice of guidance this week? Did any recurring themes emerge? What do you sense are God's invitations to you?

4. Closing exercise: offer a word of hope or encouragement to the person seated on your left. (Take time in silence to prayerfully listen before beginning the exercise.) What evidence of the Spirit's work do you glimpse in this fellow traveler? Take time to listen and savor the word that is offered to you before turning to offer a gift to someone else.

Reading for Week Five: Chapter Nine

SPIRITUAL PRACTICE: INTERCESSORY PRAYER

Paul writes, "I urge you, brothers and sisters, by our Lord Jesus Christ and by the love of the Spirit, to join me in my struggle by praying to God for me" (Romans 15:30).

This week spend time listening. Who is God bringing to mind in prayer? Think beyond a "laundry list" of needs and ask the Lord to help you pray with his heart and compassion, confident that he hears both your words and your silence. Ask the Spirit to pray through you.

In addition to praying for those you love, pray for those who make life difficult for you and for the ones you do not love (Matthew 5:43-48). Ask God to help you pray for his kingdom to come into the hearts of those who turn aside from him. Ask God to help you pray for the ones who wound and sin against you.

Pray too for the coming of the kingdom into the lives of those who weep and struggle and groan and wait. Pray for the coming of the kingdom into the world (Matthew 6:9-10).

. . . .

Week Five: Day One

CHAPTER NINE: MARA (PP. 191-193)

Scripture Meditation: John 1:9-14
Read the text several times aloud, using a translation that is unfamiliar to you. (You may wish to read from *The Message*, as Mara does.) Which word or phrase captures your attention and invites you to linger in prayer?

For Reflection and Journaling

1. Return to the theme of pondering what it means to be loved, chosen, and favored. Which practices help you meditate on the truth of God's love? Which Scripture verses remind you of the love of God? Practice declaring God's love for you every time you see your reflection.

2. Who reminds you that God loves you, sees you, and is with you? Spend time thanking God for the ways he reveals his presence through his people. Or, if this is an area of disappointment and heartache for you, offer your sorrow and longings to God.

3. What does it mean to you that Jesus was born into a world that rejected him? Dialogue with him about this.

4. Which of Mara's reflections on John 1 resonate with you? Why? What is your prayer?

Week Five: Day Two

CHAPTER NINE: *HANNAH AND MEG* (PP. 194-201)

Scripture Meditation: Mark 13:5-8, 32-37
Read the text slowly, asking the Spirit to bring it to life. What do you receive from Jesus today through his words? What thoughts, questions, or emotions are stirred as you listen? What is your prayer?

For Reflection and Journaling

1. Hannah ponders what it means to wait for the kingdom of God to be revealed, to groan, struggle, and weep even while taking comfort in the work God has already accomplished through Jesus Christ. What does it mean to sing hope and good news in a minor key? How are you longing for the kingdom to be revealed?

2. In what ways are you groaning today? For yourself? For others? For the world? Offer your groans to God.

3. Hannah writes, "No matter what it looks like from down here, you win, Lord. You win" (p. 197). In what ways do you need to be reoriented toward hope today? What helps you keep a long-range vision of hope in the midst of trials? Spend time thanking God for his promises and victory.

Week Five: Day Three

CHAPTER NINE: *NATHAN AND CHARISSA* (PP. 202-209)

Scripture Meditation: 1 John 3:2-3
Read the verses slowly and prayerfully, listening for a word or phrase that catches your attention and invites you to linger. Respond to God in prayer.

For Reflection and Journaling

1. In what ways is Charissa serving as a mirror for Nathan to see himself? What do you see about your own wrestling, resistance, sin, or places of captivity? How is the Spirit revealing truth and grace to you?

2. Nathan and Charissa are each being taken where they don't want to go. In what ways do you identify with them? Are you able to name a time in your life when you offered a costly "Here I am, Lord" prayer of surrender? What happened?

3. "God's work isn't fragile," Katherine reminds Nathan. When you feel discouraged by what appears to be a lack of progress or maturity in your life, what practices help you receive grace and persevere with hope? What concrete reminders of God's love and care would be helpful to you? Why?

4. Finish your time of reflection today by sitting in silence, using your breath prayer to center yourself in the love of God.

....

Week Five: Day Four

CHAPTER NINE: HANNAH (PP. 210-216)

Scripture Meditation: 1 John 4:9-10
Read the verses aloud a few times, taking to heart how God has demonstrated
his love. Then change the pronouns from we/us/our to I/me/my. What is
your prayer?

For Reflection and Journaling

1. Hannah ponders how to be alongside Mara and to point her to the Light
    without trying to be the Light. Is this a struggle or temptation for you in
    your relationships? In what ways? Speak with God about what you notice.

2. What types of situations or people push your buttons and agitate you?
    What might God be revealing in the agitation?

3. Hannah contemplates her struggles with scarcity and abundance, con-
    trasting the image of a pie being cut into slices and the image of a beach
    on a sunny day. In what ways do you live with a scarcity model regarding
    God's love, delight, and blessings? In what ways have you been converted
    to abundance? What is your prayer?

4. Name some of the "flowers" God has given you—the evidence of his
    love. Spend time celebrating and giving God thanks for these gifts and
    blessings. Now think of someone you envy (or someone you have envied

in the past). Spend time identifying the gifts or blessings that have been poured out on this person. Practice celebrating God's generosity, giving God thanks for the flowers that have been given to others. Ask for the grace to pray that God would lavish even more goodness on the one(s) you envy.

Week Five: Day Five

CHAPTER NINE: *MARA AND MEG* (PP. 217-223)

Scripture Meditation: Isaiah 11:1-9
Read the text slowly a couple of times. Which images capture your attention and imagination? Which promises stir and reveal your longings? What is your prayer as you wait for the kingdom of God to be fully revealed?

For Reflection and Journaling

1. Mara is surprised by unexpected blessings that appear in the midst of the mess: the broken nose and mandatory community service that result in moments of grace. Identify similar moments of grace in your own life. Then spend time thanking God for them.

2. Meg tries to be mindful of God's presence with her in the midst of challenges and heartache. What practices help you notice and name Emmanuel? If you have fallen out of the habit of praying the examen at the end of the day, try to return to it.

3. Typically, narrative texts in Scripture lend themselves more easily to praying with imagination. But Meg recognizes that Isaiah 11:1-9 is filled with images about what the kingdom of God will one day look like, so she pictures herself within the landscape described. Do any of her fears or longings resonate with you? Speak with God about what you notice.

. . . .

Week Five: Day Six

REVIEW

1. Prayerfully review your notes from this week. In what ways were you challenged? Comforted? Frustrated? Inspired? How have you seen Emmanuel revealed this week? Speak with God about what you notice.

2. What fruit do you notice from your practice of intercessory prayer this week? Spend time giving God thanks.

Week Five Group Discussion

If possible, light a candle to remind yourselves that you are in the presence of God together. Group leaders, choose a Christmas carol text for opening prayer and give everyone a copy. After reciting it in unison, sing it together.

1. Which parts of the characters' journeys this week resonated with you or challenged you? Why?

2. In what ways were you shaped or stretched by your practice of intercessory prayer this week? What fruit do you see, either in ways you were formed or in answers to prayer?

3. Recite together these words from John 1:14 (*The Message*):

    The Word became flesh and blood,
        and moved into the neighborhood.
    We saw the glory with our own eyes,
        the one-of-a-kind glory,
        like Father, like Son,
    Generous inside and out,
        true from start to finish.

Take a few minutes of silence to ponder the revealed glory and generosity of God in Christ. Then take turns offering to the group the name or first initial of someone you find it difficult to pray for. Without giving any specific details of that person's story, share a few sentences about why you struggle to pray for him or her. Let others in the group offer their prayers, both for you and for the person you identify.

Conclude your gathering time by praying for God's kingdom to come, using the words of the Lord's Prayer.

Reading for Week Six: Chapter Ten

SPIRITUAL PRACTICE: TELLING YOUR STORY

After struggling with the spiritual formation part of her final paper, Charissa realizes that she can simply write the story of her journey: the steps forward and the steps back, the longing and the fear, the resistance and the yielding, the sin and the grace. Spend time this week reflecting on and writing about your own journey. How are you moving deeper into the knowledge of God and deeper into the knowledge of yourself? How is the light shining into the darkness? What encouragement have you received along the way? (If you're walking with a group, be prepared to tell your stories during your final session together.)

....

Week Six: Day One

CHAPTER TEN: *HANNAH* (PP. 224-228)

Scripture Meditation: Galatians 6:1-2
Read the verses slowly and prayerfully. What catches your attention and calls for your response?

For Reflection and Journaling

1. Hannah is reluctant to add layers of her own baggage to Nate's. How freely do you share your burdens with others? Why? Speak with God about what you notice.

2. Do you have any deeply ingrained "emergency shut-off valves" (p. 224) within you? If so, name them. What types of situations trigger them? How is God leading you forward into healing, freedom, and maturity?

3. Bring to mind some people or situations that tempt you to begrudge God's generosity, to desire "fairness" rather than grace. How is God using these people or situations to enlarge you and conform you to Christ? Practice praying for God to pour out his kindness on them and to draw them to himself.

4. What are the physical markers or "flowers in winter" that remind you of the presence and faithfulness of God? What object could you keep visible as a reminder during this particular season of your life? (If you are participating in a group study, plan to take an object with you when you meet and share the story of its significance.)

Week Six: Day Two

CHAPTER TEN: *MARA* (PP. 229-233 AND 236-240)

Scripture Meditation: 1 Thessalonians 5:16-18
Read the verses slowly and prayerfully. Which commands are hardest for you? Why? Offer your questions, wrestling, or longings to God in prayer.

For Reflection and Journaling

1. As Mara waits for her granddaughter to be born, her mind wanders to memories of Jeremy's childhood. Identify some of the links you see between her past experiences of scarcity and her current longings and compulsions. What links can you see in your own life regarding how past struggles have affected you? Speak with God about what you see.

2. Prayerfully scan the current landscape of your life. What are you celebrating? Grieving? Questioning? Offer your honest thoughts and emotions to God in prayer.

3. In what ways are you glimpsing God's goodness and generosity to you in the midst of the heartache or mess? What's being born here? Spend time offering your gratitude.

. . . .

Week Six: Day Three

CHAPTER TEN: MEG (PP. 234-235, 241-246, AND 253-254)

Scripture Meditation: Luke 2:1-7
Read the text aloud a couple of times, imagining that you are Mary or Joseph. What thoughts and emotions are stirred as you enter their story? Offer what you notice to God in prayer.

For Reflection and Journaling

1. Is there any sin, weight, fear, or sorrow for you to unburden through prayer, journaling, or confession to a trustworthy companion? What truth needs to be voiced?

2. Katherine emails Meg some words of encouragement, commenting that it's easy to punctuate our pain with exclamation points rather than commas when we're in the midst of a trial (p. 245). Think about a time in your life when it seemed you had ended up in the wrong place. Write an account of what happened, using mostly commas. How did God reveal himself through the twists and turns of the story?

3. Meg experiences heartache as she tries to witness to Becca. What is your experience of witnessing to others? Any stories to celebrate? To grieve? Is there anyone you believe God is calling you to share your story with? How can you be in prayer for those who haven't yet received Jesus?

Week Six: Day Four

CHAPTER TEN: CHARISSA (PP. 247-248)

Scripture Meditation: 1 Thessalonians 5:23-24
Read the verses aloud, listening for a word or phrase that catches your attention and calls for your prayerful response.

For Reflection and Journaling
Give yourself space today for working on your own "two steps forward" story. In what ways have you "come to yourself"? What have you seen about your resistance and yielding? Sin and grace? Where do you glimpse God's faithfulness? It doesn't need to be a long story—just a snapshot of what you're noticing in your life with God.

. . . .

Week Six: Day Five

CHAPTER TEN: *HANNAH* (PP. 249-252)

Scripture Meditation: 1 John 3:1
Read the verse aloud a few times. Which word or phrase catches your attention and invites your prayerful response? What does it mean to know yourself as a beloved child of God?

For Reflection and Journaling

1. Who needs to hear the message of "You're not alone" right now? Find a way to encourage someone who is going through a difficult time, a way to offer "flowers in winter."

2. Katherine suggests that Hannah focus not on a "behold me" prayer but on beholding Jesus. "Don't start with your 'Here I am' to God," Katherine says. "Start with God's 'Here I am' to you" (p. 251). Why is this shift important for Hannah? Do you share anything in common with her? Speak with God about what you notice.

3. How do you (or might you) practice beholding the character and love of God? How might that regular practice affect your ability to trust him?

....

Week Six: Day Six

Review

1. Prayerfully review your notes from this week. In what ways were you challenged? Comforted? Frustrated? Inspired? How have you seen Emmanuel revealed this week? Speak with God about what you notice.

2. If your group will be sharing a "flowers in winter" object, decide what this will be.

3. Continue working on your "two steps forward" story. (If you're in a group, you'll have an opportunity to share these at the end of the study.)

Week Six Group Discussion

If possible, light a candle to remind yourselves that you are in the presence of God together. (Group leaders, if possible, bring flowers for a visual center-piece.) Begin with a few minutes of silence for breath prayer. Then read to-gether the opening stanza of "Lo, How a Rose E'er Blooming" (p. 225).

1. Name one physical object or marker that is meaningful to you in your life with God right now. If you brought an item with you, share a story about its significance. How have you glimpsed God's "Here I am" this week?

2. Read Luke 2:1-7. Then share some of your reflections from when you prayed with the text this week. Where is God inviting you to put commas in your story as you move forward with hope?

3. Spend time praying for the ones you love and long for, the ones who haven't yet said yes to the love of God in Christ. Pray for one another to have courage and opportunities to share a story about God's faithfulness with someone who needs to hear.

Reading for Week Seven: Chapter Eleven

Jesus says to his disciples, "You know that those who are regarded as rulers of the Gentiles lord it over them, and their high officials exercise authority over them. Not so with you. Instead, whoever wants to become great among you must be your servant, and whoever wants to be first must be slave of all. For even the Son of Man did not come to be served, but to serve, and to give his life as a ransom for many" (Mark 10:42-45).

In what ways can you serve others this week? Explore serving strangers as well as those you know. If you are using this guide with a group, practice serving together, either this week or at a future date. How does this discipline shape and form you in love?

. . . .

Week Seven: Day One

∞

CHAPTER ELEVEN: *CHARISSA AND MARA* (PP. 257-262)

Scripture Meditation: Philippians 2:1-11
Read the passage slowly and prayerfully. In what ways does Jesus descend? What would it mean for you to have the same mind and love as Christ? Respond to God in prayer.

For Reflection and Journaling

1. What are some practical ways you can model self-giving, humble love? Listen prayerfully for how God might be calling you to do this.

2. Think about a time in your life when God seemed hidden or when you were overwhelmed with sorrow or stress. Who are some of the people who came alongside you? Spend time thanking God for gifts of presence in the midst of pain.

3. Are there any people you have the opportunity to thank or encourage? Write a note, send an email, make a phone call, or schedule a visit.

. . . .

Week Seven: Day Two

CHAPTER ELEVEN: *HANNAH* (PP. 263-267)

Scripture Meditation: 2 Corinthians 8:9
Read the verse aloud a couple of times. How does it speak to you about Jesus' descending in love? How does the truth of his descent enlarge your gratitude? Inspire your generosity? Speak with God about what you notice.

For Reflection and Journaling

1. If you haven't yet made it a habit, practice standing in front of a mirror and declaring God's love for you. When you see others face to face this week, practice offering a prayer for them that they would know God's love in tangible ways. Is there anyone you resist praying for? Offer your resistance to God.

2. In what ways do you glimpse the Spirit's work in your life, moving you from resentment to gratitude, from despair to hope, from fear to love? Speak with God about what you see.

3. Mara describes the way her church's sanctuary is decorated. Imagine walking into a space like that. What would speak to you? Agitate you? Comfort you? Why?

4. Read the stanzas from "Lo, How a Rose E'er Blooming" aloud (p. 267). Which images catch your attention and invite your prayerful response?

....

Week Seven: Day Three

CHAPTER ELEVEN: *CHARISSA, MEG, AND MARA* (PP. 268-276)

Scripture Meditation: 1 Corinthians 13:4-7
Read the verses slowly and prayerfully, listening for a word or phrase that catches your attention. Which descriptions of love are most challenging for you? Why? Respond to God in prayer.

For Reflection and Journaling

1. In what ways are you being called to lay down your own desires in order to love someone well? Is this a costly sacrifice for you? Why or why not?

2. Bring to mind a situation in which love meant letting someone else choose his or her own way. What was that like for you? How has God kept you company in this? Do you see any ways in which God has revealed his plan and purposes through it?

3. What does it mean to "let go without giving up" (p. 270)? To let go with hope?

....

Week Seven: Day Four

CHAPTER ELEVEN: *HANNAH* (PP. 277-280)

Scripture Meditation: Luke 2:8-14
Read the text slowly, imagining yourself as a shepherd in the fields. What thoughts or emotions are stirred in you as you hear the angel's message? What is your response?

For Reflection and Journaling

1. Hannah and Nate are both surprised by an opportunity to share a gentle word of testimony with a curious tattoo artist. Have you ever had a similar experience of an unexpected opportunity to witness? If so, bring to mind the details. What did God use to open the door?

2. Hannah muses that while Becca may not want to hear her mother's testimony, she has no defenses against their prayers for her. Who joins you in prayer for the ones you love? Who do you join in prayer? Do you glimpse any fruit of your prayers? Speak with God about this.

3. Read Luke 2:8-14 slowly and prayerfully again. Using words, phrases, or images from the text, pray for others to hear and believe the good news.

. . . .

Week Seven: Day Five

CHAPTER ELEVEN: *MEG* (PP. 281-286)

Scripture Meditation: Isaiah 9:1-2
Read the verses slowly and prayerfully, listening for a word or phrase that catches your attention and calls for your response. In what ways is gloom being lifted? In what ways is light breaking into darkness? Offer God what you see.

For Reflection and Journaling

1. How are you both naming grief and rehearsing gratitude? How does (or might) this regular practice shape you and help you know Emmanuel in deeper ways?

2. As Meg does a prayerful mental inventory of the ways she has sought forgiveness from God and from Becca, she realizes she hasn't forgiven herself. Is there anything you need to forgive yourself for? Speak with God about what you see.

3. Describe the "reframing" Meg experiences as she remembers a dark and fearful moment in her life. Have you ever experienced a similar reframing of seeing how God was with you in the past? Is there such a reframing to notice and name now?

4. *Emmanuel. God with us. Even then. Even now.* What do these declarations mean to you? Respond to God in prayer.

Week Seven: Day Six

REVIEW

1. Prayerfully review your notes from this week. In what ways were you challenged? Comforted? Frustrated? Inspired? How have you seen Emmanuel revealed this week? Speak with God about what you notice.

2. Review the opportunities you took (or missed) in serving others this week. What fruit do you see? What is your prayer?

Week Seven Group Discussion

If possible this week, serve together. Or discuss potential opportunities to serve and schedule a time to do it. If you are not serving together this week, use your group time to talk about the ways you were challenged or inspired by the characters' journeys. Share any significant insights from the reflection questions. Close your time by reading Philippians 2:1-11 and discussing what it means for love to descend.

Reading for Week Eight: Chapter Twelve

SPIRITUAL PRACTICE: GRATITUDE

This week practice expressing gratitude to God and others. In what types of situations does gratitude come easily? In what types of situations is it more difficult to be thankful? Why?

What helps you remain in a posture of gratitude, regardless of circumstances?

How does the practice of gratitude shape and form you? What fruit do you see?

....

Week Eight: Day One

Chapter Twelve: *Hannah* (pp. 287-288 and 292-294)

Scripture Meditation: Mark 5:21-43

Using your imagination, enter the story as Jairus. What do you feel, think, and experience as you interact with Jesus? Offer what you notice to God in prayer.

For Reflection and Journaling

1. How does remembering God's faithfulness in the past help you trust God with the future? What stories do you need to remember? How are you being invited to trust God as you step forward?

2. What does "only believe" mean to you? Is *only* a hard word for you? Why or why not?

3. What does it mean to sing or speak with defiant exclamation points of hope?

4. Read the stanza of "Hark! The Herald Angels Sing" (p. 294). Which declarations stir your longings or hope? What is your prayer?

....

Week Eight: Day Two

CHAPTER TWELVE: *CHARISSA* (PP. 289-291)

Scripture Meditation: 2 Corinthians 3:17-18
Read the verses slowly and prayerfully. What is your response?

For Reflection and Journaling

1. Do you ever find yourself being controlled by the desire to be perfect? If so, in what ways?

2. What does "Give yourself some grace" mean to you? Where do you need to receive grace? What does grace look like?

3. Charissa names several forms of "socially acceptable" idolatry (p. 291). How have you sought to derive your significance and security apart from God? In what ways are you being called to give up control?

4. What is God using to break you free from captivity? Speak with God about what you notice.

....

Week Eight: Day Three

CHAPTER TWELVE: *CHRISTMAS EVE* (PP. 295-303)

Scripture Meditation: 1 Corinthians 13:11-13
Read the verses slowly and prayerfully. What encourages you? Challenges you? Gives you hope? Offer your longings to God.

For Reflection and Journaling

1. Identify some of the forward steps the characters have made. What evidence do you see of the Spirit's work in each of their lives?

2. What evidence of the Spirit's work do you glimpse in your life? What are you celebrating?

3. *Emmanuel, the Lord is with you. Even then, even now, even here.* Where do you glimpse the presence of Emmanuel in the past, in the present, or in the midst of trial? What is your prayer?

··

Week Eight: Day Four

∞

CHAPTER TWELVE: *CHRISTMAS DAY* (PP. 304-305)

Scripture Meditation: Jude 24-25
Read the verses aloud a couple of times. Receive them as God's promises to you. What is your prayer?

For Reflection and Journaling

1. What next steps do you hope the characters will take? Why?

2. How has community been a gift to you? What do you need from those who walk with you? What can you offer to those who walk with you?

3. Where is God inviting you to put commas in your story? Finish writing your "two steps forward" narrative.

··

Week Eight: Days Five and Six

∞

REVIEW

Prayerfully review your notes from the past eight weeks. What do you notice? Have any patterns emerged? What encourages you? For what are you most grateful? What is your prayer as you move forward?

Week Eight Group Discussion

If possible, light a candle to remind yourselves that you are in the presence of God together.

This is a day to share your own "two steps forward" narratives. Celebrate and give God thanks for what he has done as you've walked together. What next steps do you hope to take, individually and as a group?

Conclude your time by offering a benediction to one another in a circle: "Greetings, [name], favored one! The Lord is with you. Do not be afraid."

Sing a verse from a hymn or chorus that has joyful exclamations about who Christ is and what he has done.

The Sensible Shoes Series

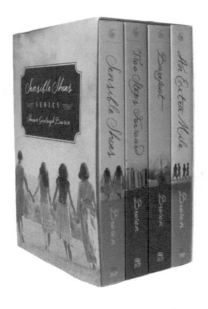

Sensible Shoes
Two Steps Forward
Barefoot
An Extra Mile